A Place to Stay

A Shelter Story

written by

Erin Gunti

illustrated by

Estelí Meza

I slammed the car door and tucked Bunny-Beth under my arm. "I don't want to stay here," I told Mama, looking up at the tall building.

"I know," Mama said softly. "But we're very lucky to have a place to stay."

I squeezed Bunny-Beth to my chest.
I didn't feel lucky. "This isn't a house,"
I whispered.

"You know what?" Mama said. "I think you're right. Looks more like a **palace** to me."

"A **palace**?" I asked.

Mama grinned. "Let's go inside and see if the queen is here."

Inside, we met a woman with short hair sitting in a tall swivel chair. Her name was Kelly.

Mama filled out some paperwork. Then Kelly said she would show us to our room on the third floor.

We passed an area with some sofas and a television on one side. Next, we walked past a room full of toys and books.

"Oh, wow," Mama exclaimed. "I believe we found the **treasure cave**."

"Is all of this for me?" I asked.

"You and all the other kids. Maybe you will make some new friends!" said Kelly.

Mama said we would visit later.

Kelly took us to the room where she said we would sleep. It was very small. "Dinner is on the first floor," she said before leaving us to unpack.

We put our bags on one of the beds. Then Mama pressed on the mattress. "A little squeaky, but it feels pretty soft."

I frowned. "That's not *my* bed."

My bed had a fluffy pink blanket and three pillows just for me. This bed had a boring grey blanket and only one pillow.

"Hmmmm," Mama replied. "You're right.
That's not your bed. In fact, that's not a bed at all."

She kicked off her shoes and
climbed onto the mattress.

"What are you doing?" I asked.

Mama took a big bounce.
She took another bounce and then another.
Her fingertips touched the ceiling.

"This isn't a bed! This is a **rocket ship** sending me straight to the stars. Do you want to touch them, too?"

Bouncing looked like fun. It took
me a few tries, but I finally touched the ceiling.

Mama looked at the clock.
"Oh, I think it's time to go downstairs for dinner."

My tummy rumbled.

"Yum! I smell spaghetti," Mama said.

The dining room was large and full of people talking loudly. Some people stood behind a counter, serving food. Others sat at tables eating.

I covered my ears. "This isn't a kitchen."

"You're right," Mama said. "This isn't a kitchen. It's a **banquet hall**."

"A **banquet hall**?" I asked.

"Yes. And, look at how many people have come from near and far to dine with us. Let's get our food and say hello, shall we?"

"Okay," I sighed.

We sat next to a woman named Alice and her two children, Grace and Andrew.

Alice let me feed Andrew a bottle. Grace and I talked about school and found out we were reading the same book!

After dinner, Mama gathered my PJs, soap
and a towel so I could have a shower.

I turned the water on, then ran my hand
under the spray. "Brrrr!" I said.

"You'll just have to wait for the water to warm up before you get in," Mama replied.

"Wait? Oh, that will never work," I said.

"And why is that?" Mama asked.

"Because we won't find warm water here," I smiled.

"Really? How will we find it?" Mama asked.

"Deep-sea diving!" I said. "Put your diving mask on."

We swam to the right. *Glug.*

We swam to the left. *Glug. Glug.*

"Over here!" I shouted.
The water was just right.

After my shower, I climbed into my **rocket ship** and snuggled with Bunny-Beth.

"Mama, this is the most comfortable rocket ship I have ever slept in," I yawned.

"I think so, too," Mama whispered,
kissing me on the cheek.
"Goodnight, sweetheart."

"Goodnight, Mama," I whispered back.

Five, four, three, two, one . . .
and we were off to sleep.

Shelters and Homelessness

Why do people stay in shelters?

The characters in this book are spending the night at a **homeless shelter**, a building that provides a place to stay for people who need it. People might have trouble finding a place to sleep at night for many different reasons. This could happen if a natural disaster like a hurricane or a flood destroys someone's home. It could also happen if someone can't pay for a place to live, maybe because they lost their job or got a big, unexpected bill. Sometimes living at home is not safe, so people have to find a new place to stay.

People who need a place to live might stay with friends or family members for a while. They might also sleep in a hotel, in their car or in a public space like a park or train station. Shelters are safe places where people can stay when they don't have somewhere else to go.

How can shelters help?

A shelter isn't just a place to sleep. Shelters can give people hot meals, warm showers and a place to wash their clothes. Some of the people who work in shelters are called **social workers**. They can help those staying in shelters find healthcare, train for new jobs or plan how to save money for a new home.

Like the characters in this book, people staying in a shelter might have a tough time getting used to living in a new place and sharing it with others. Children staying in shelters might have to go to a new school for a while. Social workers can help make these changes easier. People in the community can volunteer at shelters, helping serve food or clean the building. They can also help by giving money or by donating things shelters might need, like clothes, food, art supplies or games.

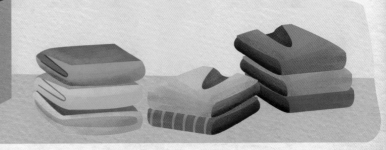

Author's Note

Working as a child abuse and neglect investigator, I was given the opportunity to provide support and resources through legal, judicial and public organizations for children and families experiencing homelessness. I wrote *A Place to Stay: A Shelter Story* to open dialogue between adults and children about childhood homelessness and to hopefully create a call to activism to support those in need. — Erin Gunti

Barefoot Books would like to thank Cristina Arias, Rayella Mojica and the clients of the Domestic Violence Action Center of Hawaii for their invaluable perspectives and thoughtful input into the creation of this book.

For my grandma, Elizabeth — E. G.
This book is dedicated to my brothers — E. M.

Barefoot Books
2067 Massachusetts Ave
Cambridge, MA 02140

Barefoot Books
29/30 Fitzroy Square
London, W1T 6LQ

Text copyright © 2019 by Erin Gunti
Illustrations copyright © 2019 by Estelí Meza
The moral rights of Erin Gunti and Estelí Meza have been asserted

First published in the United States of America by Barefoot Books, Inc
and in Great Britain by Barefoot Books, Ltd in 2019
All rights reserved

Graphic design by Sarah Soldano, Barefoot Books
Edited and art directed by Lisa Rosinsky, Barefoot Books
Reproduction by Bright Arts, Hong Kong

Printed in China on 100% acid-free paper. This book was typeset in Might Could and
Heatwave. The illustrations were done in pencils and acrylic paints, then manipulated digitally

Hardcover ISBN 978-1-78285-824-9
Paperback ISBN 978-1-78285-825-6
E-book ISBN 978-1-78285-865-2

British Cataloguing-in-Publication Data: a catalogue
record for this book is available from the British Library

Library of Congress Cataloging-in-Publication Data is available upon request

1 3 5 7 9 8 6 4 2